Äidinäiti

Grandma

Yáá

Mamm-gozh

Iaia

Anneanne

Mamale

Me

Großmutter

Grandn...

Ελληωικη

Djadda

Anyóka

Mummi

Padrina

Ba Ngoai

Babka

Mica

Dadong

Bonbonneke

Nena

Jaryi

Grand-mère

Grams

Ammamma

Chinhalmeoni

Grandmomma

Babicka

Vo-vo

Madar-bozorg

Yiayiá

お婆さん

Babaane

Aryia

Gigia

Isanaiti

Halmeoni

PHAR-MOR

Avia

Miwok

Lelang

Two
Grandmothers
To Love

Special thanks
    to my sister.....for listening;
    to my children.....for encouraging;
    to my grandchildren.....for inspiring;
    to my husband.....for everything.

HG

Also by Harriet Goldner

PLEASE, DON'T PASS OVER THE SEDER PLATE
A Haggadah for the Young and Young-at-Heart

Text copyright ©2006 by Harriet Goldner, LLC
No part of this book may be reproduced in any form without the prior written consent
of the author. Address all inquiries to P.O. Box 480003, Delray Beach, FL 33448.
Printed in Hong Kong

www.JewishFamilyFun.com

hgoldnerbooks@bellsouth.net

Illustrations by Denis Proulx
www.shangrila-studio.com

0-9779676-2-X

Two Grandmothers

To Love

By Harriet Goldner

Illustrated by Denis Proulx

Isaac and Ellie have two grandmothers.

One they call" Grammy";

and one they call" Grandma."

Both grandmothers love Isaac and Ellie.

Grammy has straight hair;

and Grandma has curly hair.

Both grandmothers love Isaac and Ellie
very much.

Grammy is Daddy's mommy;

and Grandma is Mommy's mommy.

Both grandmothers love Isaac and Ellie
very, very much.

Grammy lives in Florida;

and Grandma lives in Ohio.

Both grandmothers live in the United States;
and both of them love Isaac and Ellie
very, very, very much.

Grammy has a cat named Punum;
and Grandma has a dog named Muffy.

Both grandmothers like animals;
and both of them love Isaac and Ellie
very, very, very, very much.

Grammy likes to play golf;

and Grandma likes to play tennis.

Both grandmothers like
to play with their grandchildren;
and both of them love Isaac and Ellie
very, very, very, very, very much.

Grammy is Jewish.

She worships in a synagogue
and celebrates Jewish holidays like
Hanukkah and Passover.

Grandma is Christian.

She prays in a church
and celebrates Christian holidays
like Christmas and Easter.

Both grandmothers respect each other;

and both of them love Isaac and Ellie
very, very, very, very, very, very much.

During Hanukkah, Grammy helps
Isaac and Ellie light the candles
on the menorah at her house.

And in the spring, everyone sits down
together to enjoy the Passover Seder
with special foods and prayers.

At Christmas time, Grandma lets
Isaac and Ellie hang ornaments
on her Christmas tree.

Springtime means Easter:
laughing together on an Easter egg hunt
and sharing a specially prepared dinner.

Holidays and special days are always more fun when we are with people we love.

Imagine...........

What fun would your birthday be without other people at your celebration?

Your birthday is special.

When you have a party,
    people sing" Happy Birthday to You"
    and give you presents.

It may not be anyone else's birthday,
    but everyone there has a good
    time sharing your celebration.

All kinds of celebrations are meant to be shared with family and friends.

That's why it's fun for everyone to be together on Grammy and Grandma's special holidays.

Both grandmothers love
doing things with their families;

and both of them love Isaac and Ellie
very, very, very, very,
very, very, very much.

Grammy has straight hair,
lives in Florida with Punum,
plays golf,
and is Jewish.

Grandma has curly hair,
lives in Ohio with Muffy,
plays tennis,
and is Christian.

Most important of all.............

Both grandmothers
love Isaac and Ellie
very, very, very, very,
very, very, very, very much.

What do you call your grandmothers?

_____

What do your grandmothers call you?

_____

What are some of the things that are different about your grandmothers?

_____

_____

_____

_____

How are your grandmothers the same?
They love their grandchildren very, very, very, very, very, very, very, very much!!!

This page is for pictures of your grandmothers.